D0842614
Blackcurrant
Alice Apple
Peter
Potato
Grace Grape
Wee Willie
Water Melon

The Garden Gang
Stories and pictures by
Jayne Fisher

Other Garden Gang stories

Series 793

Penelope Strawberry and Roger Radish

Percival Pea and Polly Pomegranate

Oliver Onion and Tim Tomato

Wee Willie Water Melon and Betty Beetroot

Gertrude Gooseberry and Belinda Blackcurrant

Colin Cucumber and Patrick Pear

Peter Potato and Alice Apple

Pam Parsnip and Lawrence Lemon

Grace Grape and Robert Raspberry

Sheila Shallot and Benny Broad Bean

Avril Apricot and Simon Swede

Lucy Leek

Ladybird Books Loughborough

Lucy Leek loved lather.
She was never happier
than when she was
up to her elbows
in bubbles.
So she often
washed clean things
just for the
pleasure of it.

If it was a windy day,
that was even better
for Lucy Leek.
There was always
a chance that the
washing line might break
and then she could
do all the washing again.
The flapping of clothes
on the washing line
was music to her ears,
and the clean smell
of washing was
equally delightful
to her.

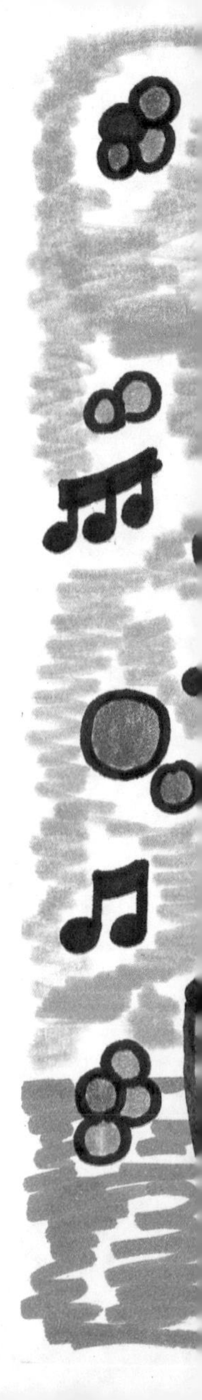

Sometimes her friends
were rather embarrassed
by her eagerness
to wash their cardigans
and scarves
as soon as they arrived.
They often had to stay
far longer than
they intended,
until their clothes
were dry enough
to put on again.

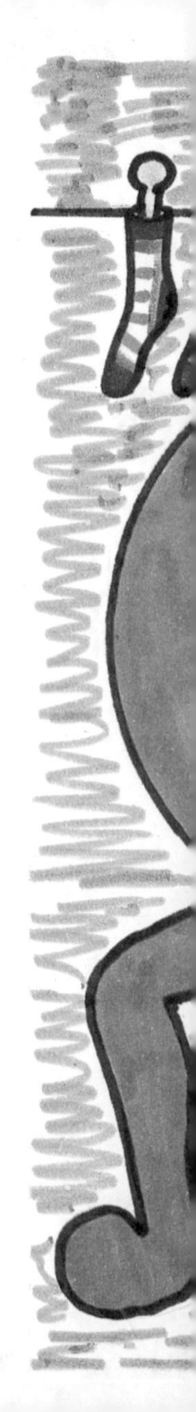

But matters came to a head
when Mrs Blackberry
sent her ten children
with a basket of goodies
for Lucy Leek.
She had been baking
all that morning
and had a few
extra biscuits
and cakes for Lucy,
who was too busy washing
to have time
to bake or cook.
Mrs Blackberry was
a good cook
and Lucy enjoyed
her food.

Mrs Blackberry
cleaned her house
all afternoon.
Then she made tea
for Mr Blackberry,
herself and the children.
But the children
did not arrive home.
As it grew dusk,
she became worried,
and hurried along
to Lucy Leek's cottage.
She hoped that
she might meet them
on the way,
but there was no sign
of her children.

Mrs Blackberry ran
up Lucy's path
and knocked on the door.
You can imagine
her relief when
the door opened
and there sat
ten little Blackberries,
eating buns and
waiting for their socks
and scarves to dry.
Of course Lucy was sorry
she had kept them
so long.
"But," she said,
"it has been a poor
drying day."

One day the Garden Gang
were having a party
in the village hall.
The food was delicious
and everyone was laughing
and chattering happily.
Suddenly Lucy Leek
appeared from nowhere
and snatched
each tablecloth
from under the
food and crockery,
splattering one or two
of the guests
with jelly and icecream.

Miss Delia Damson,
president of the Women's
Institute, was so shocked
at what had happened
that she decided
to call a meeting
to solve the
Garden Gang's problem.
''This can't go on,''
she said.
''It's so embarrassing.''
Meanwhile, Lucy Leek
skipped out joyfully
with her new pile
of dirty washing.

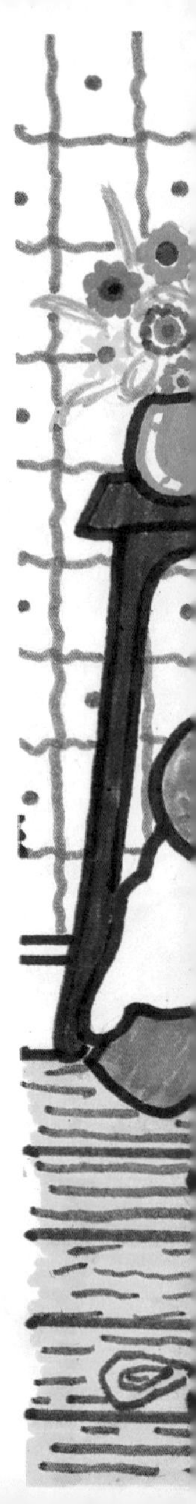

Lucy Leek soon had
those tablecloths
in hot, bubbling water.
She rubbed and scrubbed
until the cloths
were white.
She pegged them
on the washing line
and waited for them to dry.
Soon they were ready
to iron,
and in half an hour
they were crisply ironed,
folded and ready
to be returned
to the village hall.

By the time Lucy
had arrived back
at the village hall,
the Garden Gang had
made some decisions
on how to cope with
Lucy's mad desire
to wash clothes.
Delia Damson told Lucy
of their ideas
and she was delighted.
She could hardly wait
for the next day
to arrive.

When morning came,
the Garden Gang
were all very busy.
Some were tidying
Lucy's garden,
cutting her grass
and sowing seeds.
Others were cleaning
Lucy's house
and they filled her larder
with good things to eat.
In return
Lucy did all their washing.

She could now
be kept happy...

all
day
long!

Bertie Brussels Sprout

Bertie Brussels Sprout
was a great athlete.
His legs were so strong
he could easily
jump from the path
onto the compost heap.
He did this every day
to keep fit,
or so he said.

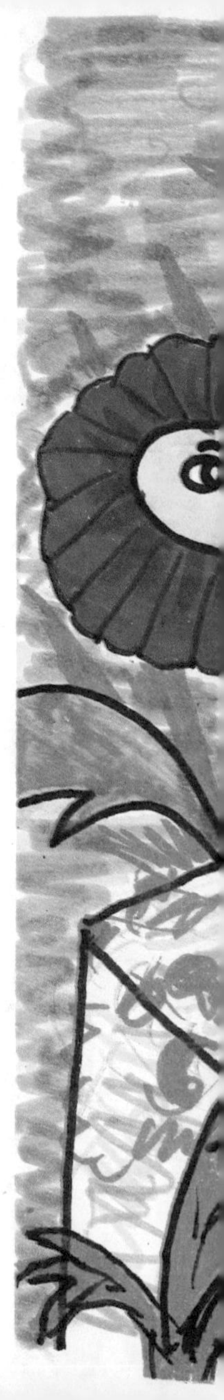

His favourite game
was sliding down
the cold-frame top,
especially on a
frosty morning,
but he also enjoyed
skating on
the frozen lily pond.

Another of his
favourite hobbies
was hurdling over
the shoe scraper
at the bottom
of the garden.
But sometimes,
when there was mud on it,
it caught on his
running shorts
and made him grubby.

One morning,
as he was jogging
down the garden,
he saw a long
metal object
shining on the grass.
Little did he know
that it was
a crochet hook
dropped by Sally,
the gardener's daughter,
the day before.

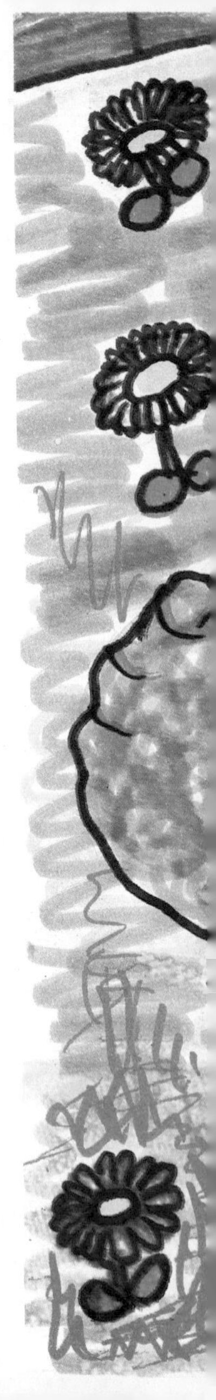

The very sight of it
made his eyes gleam.
He had visions of
himself floating
skilfully over
the pea row.
He decided now
to add pole-vaulting
to his many talents.

The Garden Gang
watched him with delight
and decided
that it would be
a good idea to hold
an inter-garden
Olympic Games.
They sent invitations
to all the
neighbouring gardens
and everyone
gladly accepted.

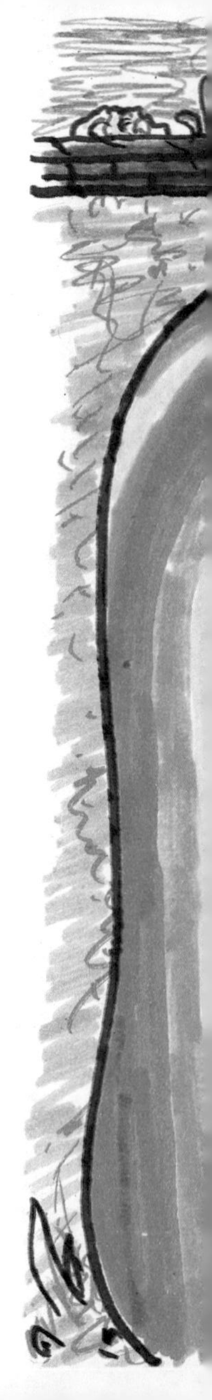

The great event
was to be held
on the fourth of June
and everyone hoped
for fine weather
because they wanted
to take part,
even if it was only
to sell tickets.

June the fourth arrived.
It was a
beautiful morning
and the sports started
with Barnaby Banana
running into the garden
carrying a lighted match
and placing it in an
upturned plant pot.
But somehow he managed
to singe his hair.
However,
he grinned bravely
at everyone
as he took
his place for
the start of the games.

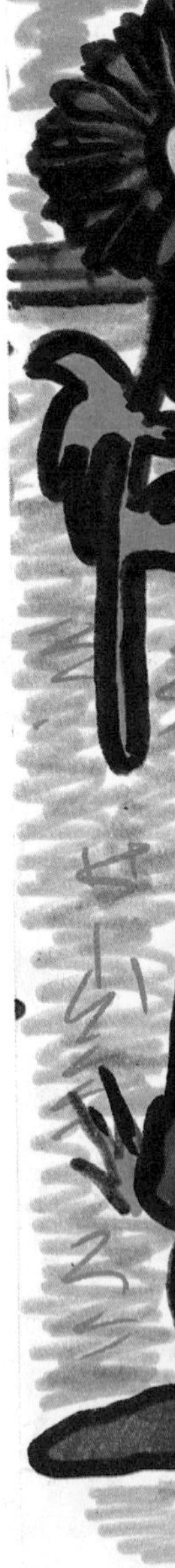

The flowers sang
a chorus from their
favourite song,
which was,
''Raindrops fall
and we grow tall,''
but they didn't get
very far with it
because they burst into
giggles at the thought of
Barnaby's singed hair.
It was a good thing
no one knew why
they were laughing
or poor Barnaby
would have been
very hurt.

The first event
was a swimming race.
Roger Radish swam
for the Garden Gang
but only came in second
because he had eaten
a huge breakfast
that morning.
Next came the gymnastics.
Percival Pea and his
grandchildren won a medal.
Polly Pomegranate gave
a brilliant performance
in the dancing competition,
and came first.
All the Garden Gang
did very well.

But the highlight
of the day was
the performance given
by Bertie Brussels Sprout.
He came first in
the high jump,
the long jump,
the hundred metres race,
the hurdles race,
the marathon race
and his new-found hobby
of pole-vaulting,
in which he jumped
a terrific height.
He went home
very tired
but *very* happy.

He slept that night
with his gold medal...

under
his
pillow!

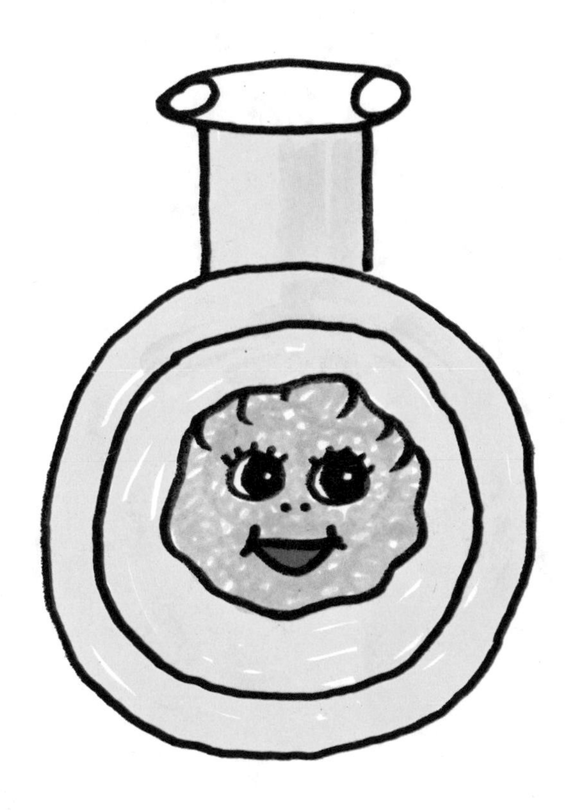

Bertie Brussels Sprout
Paul Pumpkin
Mark Marrow
Gertrud
Gooseberr
Tim Tomato
Avril Apricot
Patrick Pear